My dearest puppy, Storm,

I hope this letter reaches you safe and sound. You have been so brave since you had to flee from the evil wolf Shadow.

Do not worry about me. I will hide here until you are strong enough to return and lead our pack. For now you must move on – you must hide from Shadow and his spies. If Shadow finds this letter I believe he will try to destroy it . . .

Find a good friend – someone to help finish my message to you. Because what I have to say to you is important. What I have to say is this: you must always

Please don't feel lonely. Trust in your friends and all will be well.

Your loving mother,

Canista

Sue Bentley's books for children often include animals, fairies and wildlife. She lives in Northampton and enjoys reading, going to the cinema, relaxing by her garden pond and watching the birds feeding their babies on the lawn. At school she was always getting told off for daydreaming or staring out of the window – but she now realizes that she was storing up ideas for when she became a writer. She has met and owned many cats and dogs and each one has brought a special kind of magic to her life.

Sue Bentley

Magic Puppy

Friendship Forever

Illustrated by Angela Swan

PUFFIN

To Pash – gorgeous, charming spotty girl . . .

except for the snail-crunching!

PUFFIN BOOKS

Published by the Penguin Group
Penguin Books Ltd, 80 Strand, London WC2R 0RL, England
Penguin Group (USA) Inc., 375 Hudson Street, New York, New York 10014, USA
Penguin Group (Canada), 90 Eglinton Avenue East, Suite 700, Toronto, Ontario, Canada M4P 2Y3
(a division of Pearson Penguin Canada Inc.)
Penguin Ireland, 25 St Stephen's Green, Dublin 2, Ireland (a division of Penguin Books Ltd)
Penguin Group (Australia), 250 Camberwell Road, Camberwell, Victoria 3124, Australia
(a division of Pearson Australia Group Pty Ltd)
Penguin Books India Pvt Ltd, 11 Community Centre, Panchsheel Park, New Delhi – 110 017, India
Penguin Group (NZ), 67 Apollo Drive, Rosedale, North Shore 0632, New Zealand
(a division of Pearson New Zealand Ltd)
Penguin Books (South Africa) (Pty) Ltd, 24 Sturdee Avenue, Rosebank,
Johannesburg 2196, South Africa

Penguin Books Ltd, Registered Offices: 80 Strand, London WC2R 0RL, England

puffinbooks.com

First published 2009
1

Text copyright © Sue Bentley, 2009
Illustrations copyright © Angela Swan, 2009
All rights reserved

The moral right of the author and illustrator has been asserted

Set in Bembo
Made and printed in England by Clays Ltd, St Ives plc

British Library Cataloguing in Publication Data
A CIP catalogue record for this book is available from the British Library

ISBN: 978-0-141-32478-4

Prologue

Storm padded slowly along the shore of
the frozen lake. Snow clouds gathered in
the sky above the young silver-grey wolf.

Suddenly, a piercing howl echoed in
the frosty air.

'Shadow!' Storm gasped, trembling
with fear.

The fierce lone wolf, who had attacked
the Moon-claw pack and left his mother

injured, was close by. Storm must disguise himself, and quickly!

There was a dazzling gold flash and a fountain of golden sparks that reflected off the icy surface of the lake. Where the wolf cub had stood, there now crouched a rare Akita puppy, with fluffy fawn-and-cream fur, pricked ears and big midnight-blue eyes.

Storm turned and raced towards some ice-covered rocks. His little puppy heart beat fast as his paws skidded, and he tumbled over and over in his haste.

'Storm. In here!' called a deep velvety growl.

'Mother?' Storm whined, leaping to his feet and plunging towards the shelter of the ice cave.

The she-wolf was lying curled up just

inside the entrance. In the dim light,
the tiny puppy saw her lift her head and
her golden eyes softened with affection.
Storm's whole body wriggled and his tail
twirled as he crept close and licked her
muzzle in greeting.

Canista nuzzled her disguised-cub's
fluffy fur. 'It is good to see you again,
my son. But you have returned at a
dangerous time. Shadow is searching for
you. He wants to lead the Moon-claw
pack.'

Storm's midnight-blue eyes flared with
sorrow and anger. 'He has already killed
my father and litter brothers. I will face
Shadow and force him to leave our land!'

'Bravely said. But he is too strong for
you and I am still weak from his poisoned
bite and cannot help you fight him. Go

to the other world. Use this disguise to hide. Return when your magic is stronger. Then, together, we will fight Shadow.' Canista's head flopped back tiredly as she finished speaking.

Storm nodded slowly. He did not want to leave her, but he knew his mother was right. He leaned forward and huffed out a warm puppy breath, which glistened with thousands of tiny sparks. The healing mist whirled round Canista's wounded paw and then sank into her fur, but before Storm could complete the healing a thunderous snarl sounded outside the cave.

Mighty paws with iron-hard claws began scraping at the ice.

'Go, Storm! Save yourself,' Canista growled urgently.

Storm threw one last glance at his mother. His fluffy fawn-and-cream fur ignited with gold sparks. He whined softly as he felt the power building inside him.

The golden light around him glowed brightly. And grew brighter still . . .

Chapter ONE

Tyra Carson shivered in the early morning chill, as the fireman helped her and her mum climb out of the rowing boat.

Her dad was unloading cases and dumping them on the road out of reach of the flood water. 'Thank goodness Pam and Mark have offered to let us stay until our house is fit to live in again.'

Tyra wrapped her arms round herself, glad to be safely on dry land. She was a bit nervous of meeting Pam and Mark Baker, who she hadn't seen for ages. They were old college friends of her parents and lived at the other end of town. Tyra remembered that they had a daughter called Rachel.

Tyra saw a car draw up at the top of the hill. It stopped and two people got out.

'Here's Pam and Mark!' cried Mrs Carson, waving.

'Right then, folks. I'll leave you to it,' the fireman said cheerily, climbing back into the boat. He winked at Tyra. 'You take care now, young lady.'

Tyra managed a wobbly smile. 'I will. Thanks,' she called, as he rowed away to rescue another family.

It had finally stopped raining, but the main road was under nearly a metre of water after the river had burst its banks. Tyra tried hard not to think of their house with its flooded downstairs rooms and ruined furniture.

A man in a canoe paddled past. He had

a cat in a pet carrier balanced on his lap.
Tyra grinned, feeling cheered by the sight.

Her mum saw her looking and smiled.
'That's one lucky moggy, isn't it?' She
linked arms with Tyra and they trudged
up the steep hill together towards the
Bakers' car.

Pam Baker greeted them with hugs and

kind words. 'You poor things! You must
be frozen. Let's get you up to the house!'

Her husband, Mark, helped load the
suitcases into the car before they set off.
After the short drive, Pam went up the
front drive and opened the house door. 'I
hope you'll treat this place as your home,'
she said kindly, ushering them inside.

'That goes for me too,' said Mark. 'And
if there's anything you need, you only
have to ask.'

'Thanks. We really appreciate this,' Tyra's
dad said.

'What are friends for?' Pam said. 'It
must have been awful to wake up and
find river water flooding into the house.
Thank goodness the emergency services
were soon on the scene.'

'It was really scary,' Tyra agreed. 'I'm so

glad we're here now.'

'Me too,' said Pam. 'I'll cook some bacon and eggs and make a pot of tea. Things always look brighter after some hot food. Maybe you'd like to take your things upstairs and get settled in? Mark will help, won't you?' she said to her husband.

'Sure thing,' Mark said brightly. 'Follow me, troops.'

Tyra felt herself relaxing as she followed Mark and her mum and dad upstairs. She'd forgotten how nice the Bakers were.

'Where's Rachel?' Tyra's mum asked.

'She's just popped down the road to say goodbye to one of her friends, who's going on holiday,' Mark explained, opening bedroom doors. 'She won't be

long.' After dumping the cases, he left Tyra
and her parents to unpack and settle in.

Tyra had been put in a small back
bedroom. 'Pam's made it very welcoming,
hasn't she?' her mum said, placing a pile
of clothes on the bed.

Tyra looked around. There were
colourful posters on the walls and a
bookcase piled with toys and games. The
stripy pink duvet cover, pillow cases and
matching curtains looked new.

'It's really nice,' Tyra agreed. She looked
towards the case, which was now almost
empty. 'Is Jemima in the other suitcase?'
Jemima was a gorgeous china doll with
golden hair and a blue silk dress. She
belonged to Shelly, Tyra's best friend, who
had recently moved away. Tyra and Shelly
had arranged for Tyra to look after

Jemima, so that they had a good excuse
for making sure that their mum and dads
would let them meet up again.

Her mum frowned. 'I'm not sure.
Which one did you put her in?'

'Me? I thought *you* packed her!' Tyra
exclaimed.

'Oh dear.' Her mum looked puzzled.

'I checked your bedroom, but Jemima wasn't on your bed. So I assumed you'd already packed her.'

Tyra had a horrible sinking feeling. 'I think I might have left Jemima sitting on the sofa when I went to bed! She'll be soaked through!'

'Well, it can't be helped now. We'll have to search for her in a few days' time, once the water's gone down.'

'Shelly's going to be so upset with me when she finds out. Maybe she won't want to meet up again now,' Tyra said miserably.

Mrs Carson ruffled her daughter's light-brown hair and dropped a kiss on her head. 'Of course she will. Shelly will understand that it was an accident. You didn't leave Jemima at the house on purpose.'

Tyra hoped that her mum was right. Shelly adored Jemima, who was very old and had belonged to her grandma.

After her mum finished putting clothes away and went downstairs, Tyra sank glumly on to the bed. She thought of all the fun she and Shelly used to have. A wave of loneliness washed over her as she wished that her best friend hadn't moved so far away.

Suddenly, the bedroom door flew open and a slim dark-haired girl burst in. 'Oh, I forgot you were going to be in my room!' she exclaimed.

'Hi . . . um, Rachel,' Tyra said distractedly.

'Hiya, Tyra! I was at the same party as you a couple of weeks ago. It was fun, wasn't it?' Rachel said with a bright smile.

Tyra frowned. She vaguely remembered Rachel having been at a party she'd gone to, but she'd been too busy having fun with Shelly to take much notice.

'We can get to know each other properly now that you're staying here,' Rachel said.

'Yeah, I guess so,' Tyra murmured, shrugging. Leaving Jemima behind in the flooded house had been the final straw. She felt too downcast to make much effort to be friendly to someone she hardly knew at the moment.

Rachel flushed and her smile wavered. 'Don't sound too keen, will you?' she grumbled. 'I've only totally changed my entire room round for you! How long are you staying here for, anyway? I don't fancy camping out in our loft forever.'

'I don't know. Until our house dries
out a bit, I expect,' Tyra told her gloomily.
*If I had my way, we'd be out of here and back
home tomorrow*, she thought.

'Rachel?' Pam's cheerful voice called up
the stairs. 'Did you tell Tyra that breakfast's
ready?'

'Yeah! We're just coming!' Rachel
answered. She turned to Tyra. 'You heard
that, right?' she said, before flouncing out
and stomping downstairs.

'Oh, great,' Tyra breathed a heavy sigh. Rachel obviously hated her for pinching her bedroom and seemed to have completely changed her mind about wanting her to stay there. Tyra found herself dreading the next few weeks.

She stood up, intending to go downstairs when a dazzling flash of bright golden light lit up the entire bedroom. Blinded for a moment, Tyra rubbed her eyes. When she could see again, she saw a tiny puppy with a round face, pointed ears and the fluffiest fawn-and-cream fur she had ever seen. It blinked at her with enormous midnight-blue eyes.

'Can you help me, please?' it woofed.

Chapter
TWO

Tyra gaped at the tiny puppy in
astonishment. Was this one of Rachel's
toys? She thought Rachel might have
been a bit too old for a talking toy.

'Hello. Aren't you gorgeous? I've never
seen a puppy like you before. You're
almost like a fluffy little teddy bear! Who
do you belong to?' she wondered aloud.
The puppy's furry brow wrinkled in a

frown. 'I do not belong to anyone. I am Storm of the Moon-claw pack. What is your name?'

Tyra did a double take. 'You-you really c-can talk!' she gabbled.

Storm nodded. Despite his tiny size he didn't seem to be all that scared of her. He was looking up at her expectantly, with his ears pricked, and Tyra realized that he was waiting for her to reply.

'I'm Tyra. Tyra Carson. I'm staying here
with my mum and dad because our house
is flooded.' She bent down and tried to
make herself smaller so as not to alarm
this amazing puppy. She still couldn't
quite believe this was happening to her
and she didn't want Storm to run away.

Storm bowed his little round head.
'I am honoured to meet you, Tyra.'

'Um . . . me too.' Tyra blinked as she
remembered something that Storm had
just said. 'What's the Moon-claw pack?'

'It is the wolf pack once led by my
father and mother,' Storm told her
proudly in a gruff little bark. His big blue
eyes lit up with anger. 'Shadow, an evil
lone wolf, killed my father and three litter
brothers and wounded my mother. He
wants to lead our pack, but the others will

not follow him while I am alive.'

'Hold on! Did you say *wolf*? But you're a tiny pu—'

'Stay back, please,' Storm ordered, backing away.

As Tyra straightened up, there was another dazzling bright flash and the air fizzed with a cloud of gold sparks that drifted harmlessly around her and fell to the carpet.

'Oh!' Tyra rubbed her eyes and when she could see again she noticed that the tiny fluffy fawn-and-cream puppy had gone. In its place there stood a powerful young silver-grey wolf with thick fur and paws that seemed too big for its body. Its neck ruff gleamed with big golden sparkles, like yellow jewels.

Tyra eyed the wolf's large sharp teeth

and strong muscles. 'Storm?'

'Yes, it is me, Tyra. I will not harm you. Do not be afraid,' Storm growled softly.

But before Tyra had time to get used to the amazing young wolf, there was a final gold flash and Storm reappeared as a tiny, helpless fawn-and-cream puppy.

'Wow! You really are a wolf!' Tyra exclaimed. 'That's a brilliant disguise!'

Storm began to tremble all over and his bushy little tail drooped. 'It will not save me if Shadow uses his magic to find me. I must hide. Will you help me?' he whined.

Tyra's soft heart went out to the terrified puppy. She picked Storm up and stroked his soft little head. His fur was softer than cotton wool and smelled of fresh air. 'Of course I'll help. You can live with me in my bedroo–' She stopped as

she remembered where she was – 'Oh,
I might not be allowed to keep you. I
don't know how my parents' friends' feel
about pets. And I'm staying in Rachel's
bedroom. Rachel's their daughter.'

'I understand. Thank you for your
kindness. I will find someone else, who
can help me,' Storm woofed politely,
wriggling to be put down.

'Hold on a minute,' Tyra said, shifting her grip, so that Storm settled in her arms again. She wasn't ready to lose her new friend that easily. Before he'd arrived she'd been feeling really miserable, especially as Rachel had done a sudden about-turn and now didn't seem to even want her there. 'There must be something I can do. Let's go and talk to my mum and dad. They usually have good ideas. I can't wait to see their faces when I tell them about you!'

Storm twisted round to look up at her, his little face serious. 'No, Tyra. You cannot tell anyone my secret!' he warned. 'You must promise me!'

Tyra felt disappointed that she couldn't share her news about the magical little puppy, but if it would help to keep Storm safe from his enemy, she was prepared to agree. 'OK. Cross my heart. Your secret's safe with me. But I'm still not sure what to do about keeping you.'

'Keeping who?' said her dad as he poked his head round the door. 'I came to see where you'd got . . . Goodness me. Where on earth did that puppy come from?'

Tyra almost jumped out of her skin. She'd been so busy talking to Storm that she hadn't heard her dad coming up the stairs. It looked like her secret was out!

She gulped and did some quick thinking. 'I . . . um, found him just after we . . . er, got out of the boat,' she fibbed. 'Storm must have been swept away in the floods and now he's completely lost. *Which is true in a way*, she thought. She had a sudden brainwave. 'I . . . I really wanted to look after him, especially as I'm missing Shelly so much and Jemima got left behind. But I didn't think that you and Mum would let me keep him. So I . . . um, smuggled Storm in here, under my coat,' she said, looking up at him with what she hoped was a convincingly guilty expression.

Her dad raised his eyebrows. 'Well, you're certainly full of surprises, Tyra Carson! I didn't notice you picking up any soggy stray pup and stowing it away in the car!'

'I know. I was super-quick. Sorry. It was a bit sneaky, wasn't it?' she said, chewing her lip.

'You can say that again!' her dad sighed, but there was a twinkle in his eye. 'I don't know what Pam and Mark are going to make of this. I suppose we'd better go downstairs and see.'

'Storm's adorable, though, isn't he?' Tyra insisted. 'Have you ever seen such a fluffy ball of fur? He's so soft. Why don't you stroke him and see?'

Her dad reached out and rubbed Storm under his chin. Storm wagged his bushy tail and leaned his head forward in enjoyment. Mr Carson's face softened and he smiled. 'Storm's a really unusual pup, all right. I wonder what breed he is. And I like his name. It really suits him.'

'So will you ask Pam and Mark if he can stay, for me?' Tyra said in her best pleading voice. 'I'll look after him and take him for walks and buy dog food with my pocket money. And Storm can come home with us, when our house is all dried out.'

Her dad gave her a rueful grin. 'You've really fallen for that little puppy, haven't you?'

Tyra nodded. 'I already love him to bits!'

'Well, I suppose I could put in a word for you, but if Pam and Mark say no, there'll be no arguments.'

Chapter
THREE

'Of course you can keep him until
someone comes forward to claim him,'
Pam said the moment Tyra finished
explaining about Storm. 'I don't mind at
all. What about you, Mark?'

'It's fine by me. You're the boss!' Mark
joked.

Tyra beamed at them both. 'Thanks
so much!' She wrapped her arms round

Storm and cuddled his fluffy little body.

Storm gave a tiny delighted woof and leaned up to lick her nose with his warm pink tongue. 'That is good! This is a safe place. I like it here.'

Tyra stiffened. Storm had just spoken to her in front of everyone else!

She expected cries of wonder and astonishment from the grown-ups and Rachel, but nothing happened. Storm's midnight-blue eyes glinted with mischief as he looked up at Tyra. 'Only you can hear me speak,' he yapped.

Tyra smiled affectionately at her new little friend. Storm was full of surprises. She wondered what else he could do.

Her mum bent down to stroke the tiny puppy's fluffy fawn-and-cream fur. 'Storm seems pleased about being able to stay. It's almost as if he understands every word we say!'

Tyra hid a smile. If only her mum knew how right she was.

Rachel had been silent up until now. Her dark hair had fallen forward to hide her face as she sat at the kitchen table munching toast. 'Don't bother to ask me, will you? No one cares what I think,' she muttered, scowling.

Pam looked at her daughter in surprise. 'But I thought you'd love the idea of having a puppy in the house. You're always going on about wanting a dog.'

'Yeah! And I've never been allowed to have one, have I?' Rachel complained. 'So how come, it's suddenly OK for Tyra?'

Tyra's mum looked a bit embarrassed. 'If this is going to be a problem, maybe we should just phone the pet care centre and take Storm there,' she said quietly.

'No, we can't!' Tyra burst out. 'I've already promised Storm that . . . I mean, I've promised myself that I'll take care of Storm. He *has* to stay with me!'

'Now, Tyra, be reasonable. Remember what I said? This isn't up to you,' her dad warned gently.

Tyra swallowed. She made a big effort

to stay quiet in case she made things worse. But she hoped like mad that her parents' friends wouldn't change their minds because of Rachel's objections.

But she needn't have worried.

'Rachel, be fair –' Pam shook her head slowly and reached out to ruffle her daughter's dark hair – 'it'll be nice for Tyra to have a puppy for company while she's staying here. All this upheaval with the floods is very upsetting.'

'I suppose so,' Rachel admitted grudgingly.

Tyra heaved a huge sigh of relief. Storm was staying!

She turned to Rachel with a grateful smile, but the other girl was staring fixedly at the table again and didn't notice. Tyra could see that Rachel's face

was bright red and her lips were pressed
together in a thin line.

She tensed as she saw that the other
girl seemed furious. She might have given
in, but Rachel wasn't at all happy that
Tyra had been allowed to keep Storm.

Tyra avoided looking across the table
at Rachel as she quickly finished her
breakfast. Storm was lying next to her

feet, with his wet black nose resting
between his fluffy front paws.

'Thanks very much, Pam,' Tyra said
politely. She got up and carried her plate
over to the sink and then turned to her
dad. 'Is it OK if I take Storm for a walk?'

At the word 'walk' Storm jumped to
his feet, looking bright-eyed and wagging
his creamy bushy tail.

'Course it is. Storm looks pretty eager
to go out,' her dad replied.

'The old Recreation Ground's quite
near. We went there once, when you
visited. Do you remember where it is?'
asked Mark.

Tyra nodded.

Her dad fished in his pocket for some
coins. 'Here you are. That should tide you
over until you get your pocket money at

the weekend. Why don't you buy a few tins of dog food after you've been to the Rec?'

'I will. Thanks, Dad.' Tyra went into the hall with Storm at her heels. 'See you later, everyone,' she called.

'Bye!' called a chorus of voices.

Tyra noticed that Rachel didn't join in. As soon as she and Storm were alone,

Tyra breathed a sigh of relief. 'Phew! I'm glad to get out of there. Did you see Rachel? She was giving me mega-dirty looks all through breakfast.'

Storm twisted his head round to look up at her with alert blue eyes. 'Why would she do that?' he woofed curiously.

Tyra shrugged. 'Probably because she's mad about not getting her own way. She was furious that I was allowed to keep you, because she's not allowed to have a puppy. How come Rachel's so grumpy when her mum and dad are really nice?'

Storm blinked. 'I did not think that Rachel looked angry. I thought she looked a bit upset.'

'Really?' Tyra asked. 'Anyway, let's forget about her for now.' She looked towards a side street. 'I think we go down there and turn left to get to the Rec.'

Storm's furry little brow wrinkled in a frown. 'What is a Rec?'

'It's a big field with a bowling green and kids' playground and stuff. You can have a good run about.'

Storm's bright eyes sparkled. 'My favourite thing!' he woofed happily.

Tyra smiled at the little puppy's eagerness.

She and Storm walked to the end of the road and then turned into a long tree-lined avenue. On one side, the row of houses stopped at the edge of a large open space. There was a small fenced area near the road, containing swings and a slide, and a flower bed with cheerful tulips and daffodils.

'Ruff! Ruff!' Storm kicked up his heels

and took off across the grass.

Tyra watched him dashing around and snuffling up all the exciting smells.

As she wandered along, enjoying the fresh smell of cut grass, Storm gambolled after her, his tail twirling happily. Tyra found a crisp packet and crumpled it up into a tight ball and she and Storm played a game of throw and catch.

Storm was panting hard, his little pink tongue lolling out, by the time they were

wandering back along the path towards the road.

'We'll go and buy you some food now. I bet you're feeling hungry, aren't you?' Tyra asked.

'Yes. I am!' Storm woofed happily.

As Tyra got closer to the children's playground, she noticed two older boys messing about on the slide. One of them was tall and tough-looking, with a thin face and short sandy hair, and looked about fourteen. The other one was shorter and stocky with brown hair.

As they spotted Tyra they nudged each other and stood up.

'Uh-oh,' Tyra said nervously, slowing her steps.

Chapter
FOUR

'Is something wrong, Tyra?' Storm yapped,
pricking his ears.

Before Tyra could answer, one of the
boys called to her. 'My mate wants to
have a look at that pooch! Ed reckons he's
lost a dog that looks just like that.'

Tyra's skin prickled with alarm as both
boys got down from the slide and stood
facing her. She hung back, trying to

decide whether to ignore them and hurry
past. But she knew that the older boys
could easily catch her up if they wanted to.

Tyra lifted her chin, and tried to look
braver than she felt as she and Storm
went towards them. 'I think you've made
a mistake,' she said, and then she lowered
her voice to whisper, 'I don't trust these
boys. Stay close to me, Storm.'

Storm nodded, his midnight-blue eyes narrowing warily.

The boy called Ed, wearing expensive jeans and trainers, stood waiting as Tyra approached. He turned to Storm and crouched down, slapping his thighs to encourage Storm to jump up and be stroked. 'Come here, boy. Come on . . . er, Buster!'

'His name's not Buster. It's Storm,' Tyra said.

'Says you,' Ed sneered. 'What are you doing with *my* dog?'

Tyra's heart began to thud painfully, but she held her ground. 'He isn't yours. He's mine!'

Ed's thin face twisted in a grin. 'Prove it! What breed is he then?' He glanced at his friend. 'I bet she doesn't know, Dale.'

Dale grinned at Ed.

Tyra realized that the boy was right. She didn't know what breed Storm was. What she *did* know was that there was no way that these two bullies were getting their hands on her tiny friend. She started to try and walk round the boys in a wide circle, but Ed dodged in front of her.

'Storm – I mean Buster – is a rare Akita puppy. How would I know that, if he didn't belong to me?' he said triumphantly.

Tyra couldn't care less, but she wisely kept silent.

'Ed knows loads about dogs,' Dale informed her. 'You'd better hand that puppy over.'

Tyra's mouth was dry. Both boys looked strong and mean. 'You're not having Storm. He doesn't belong to you, so there!' she gulped. 'Come on, Storm! We're leaving.'

Ed moved again to stand in her way. 'I don't think so,' he drawled.

'You can't stop me!' Tyra tried to edge round Ed. 'Run, Storm!'

But Ed moved like lightning. Shoving Tyra aside, he reached down to grab the tiny puppy.

'Oh!' Tyra gasped as she stumbled against the metal slide, banging her knee hard.

Storm yelped as Ed grasped him tightly round his middle and swept him under one arm. Storm's dangling back legs peddled frantically as he struggled to get away. A soft growl rumbled in the tiny puppy's throat and his big blue eyes lit up

with anger.

Tyra felt a faint warm tingling sensation down her spine, but she hardly noticed it for the pain in her sore knee.

'You rotten bully! Leave Storm alone!' she screamed.

'Make me!' Ed crowed.

Dale was starting to look uncomfortable. 'Maybe we should leave it, Ed. I think that girl's hurt.'

'She's just faking –' Ed stopped and then a look of astonishment crossed his face – 'What's happening?' he yelled, gazing down at his hands in horror. They swelled up until they looked like a pair of inflated purple rubber gloves! 'I must be allergic to that pup's fur or something!'

Ed thrust Storm back at Tyra. 'Here! You hold him!'

Tyra gathered Storm close, protectively, while trying to balance on one leg.

'Hey! What's going on?' called a girl's voice.

Tyra saw Rachel in the distance. She was frowning furiously as she started to run. 'Why don't you clear off and pick on someone your own size!' she shouted to Dale and Ed.

'Huh! Some people can't take a joke!'

Ed said. 'C'mon, Dale.' The boys slouched off with Ed still flexing his purple swollen hands.

As Rachel drew nearer, Tyra's legs gave way and she sank down on to the flat end of the slide. Now that the excitement was over, she felt all sick and wobbly and her knee was throbbing like mad.

'Thank you for sticking up for me, Tyra. You were very brave,' Storm barked gratefully, and then his fluffy little face creased in concern. 'But you are hurt! I will make you better.'

Time seemed to stand still. Tyra felt another warm tingling sensation down her spine, but this time it was much stronger. Bright gold sparks ignited in Storm's fluffy fawn-and-cream fur and his pointed ears crackled and fizzed with electricity.

Storm rested a paw on her injured knee and a glittering golden mist flowed from it. As the sparkles swirled around her, forming a sort of magical bandage, Tyra felt the pain grow hot and increase for a moment and then drain away, as if she had poured it down a sink.

'Thanks, Storm. My knee's all better now.' She smiled at her friend. 'You certainly taught that horrible Ed a lesson! Those purple hands looked really awful!'

'The magic will not last long and his hands will not be harmed.' Storm put his head on one side and showed his sharp little teeth in a doggy grin. 'Did you say that we were going to buy some food?'

Tyra laughed at his cheeky expression. 'I certainly did and I think you deserve a treat too. How about a yummy dog chew?'

Storm woofed and licked his lips.

Seconds later, Rachel came running up as time returned to normal. 'Dale and Ed go to my school. They're always in trouble. Are you OK, Tyra?' she puffed.

Tyra nodded. Rachel must not have been able to see the magic that Storm had just done. 'I'm fine now, thanks. I wish Shelly could have been here with me. She can be pretty tough sometimes. Those boys wouldn't have dared to pick on me and Storm.'

Rachel's face fell. 'I came to see if you wanted me to show you where the shops are, but I guess you don't need *my* help.' She turned round and marched back across the Rec.

Tyra stared after her. Now what was wrong? Rachel was so touchy. She just couldn't work her out. 'Come on, Storm. Let's find those shops,' she said.

Storm glanced over his shoulder at Rachel, his dewy eyes troubled, before he scampered after Tyra.

Back inside Pam and Mark's kitchen, Tyra

forked dog food into a bowl. With an eager woof, Storm began chomping it up.

The warm room still smelled faintly of fried bacon and coffee. Her mum and dad were sitting at the table reading newspapers. The radio was on in the background.

'Did you and Storm have a good walk?' her mum asked, as Tyra sat down with them. 'Rachel went to find you. Did you see her?'

'Yeah. We saw her and then she went off by herself. I suppose she had something else to do,' Tyra replied. She decided not to mention anything about the incident with Dale and Ed. She hated people who told tales.

The local news came on the radio and they all stopped talking and listened. After the newsreader finished speaking, Tyra's dad smiled. 'It seems that the water level's falling fast. We'll soon be able to go back to the house and inspect the damage.'

'Maybe we can find Jemima and bring her back here to give her a wash and brush up,' her mum added.

Tyra felt a guilty pang. Since Storm had arrived, she hadn't felt all that lonely for her best friend. But at the mention of Shelly, she started worrying again about what Shelly was going to say about the lost doll.

Chapter
FIVE

'I think we'd better leave Storm here,'
Tyra's mum decided, a couple of days
later. 'We can't have him paddling about
in all that mess and getting filthy.'

They were borrowing Pam and Mark's
car to drive back to the house. Tyra
wasn't looking forward to seeing it for
the first time after the floods, but she had
explained about Jemima to Storm and he

had offered to help Tyra look for her.

'Storm will be fine here with us,' said Pam. She smiled at Tyra. 'I could ask Rachel to take him out for a walk when she gets back from school, if you like?'

'That would be OK,' Storm woofed gently to Tyra.

Tyra was surprised that Storm didn't seem to mind Rachel, even though Tyra wasn't sure how to take her. One minute Rachel seemed friendly and the next she was all prickly and sulky. It was most confusing.

Tyra decided that there was no way she was leaving Storm behind, but she couldn't see how she could take him with her. She bent down and pretended to fiddle with her shoe.

'What shall I do? I really want you to

come too,' she whispered to him.

Storm's big blue eyes were thoughtful. 'Tell them that you are going upstairs to fetch something,' he yapped.

'OK. Tyra wasn't sure what he was planning, but she stood up and did as he asked. 'I'll only be a minute. I'll meet you in the car,' she called to her mum and dad, heading towards the stairs.

'Have you got a bag I could hide in?' Storm woofed as he ran up the stairs beside her.

'Oh, I get it! Good idea!' Tyra went into her bedroom and grabbed an empty shoulder bag she'd brought with her. She usually used it for school books, but her school was closed indefinitely because of the floods.

Tyra opened the bag and Storm

jumped straight inside. 'You'll have to keep very quiet and stay out of sight. If Mum and Dad notice you, they'll make me leave you in the car,' she warned.

Storm's little muzzle wrinkled in a grin. 'Do not worry. I will use my magic, so that only you will be able to see and hear me.'

'You can make yourself invisible?
Cool! There's no problem then.' She had
a brainwave. 'I'll tell Pam that you're up
here having a nap, then if Rachel comes
looking for you when she gets home
from school, we can always say that you
were hiding or something.'

Storm nodded. 'That is good.'

Tyra shouldered her bag, with her tiny
friend inside, and went outside to the car.

Twenty minutes later, Tyra and Storm
stood beside her mum and dad in the
kitchen doorway of their house.

Tyra was stunned. She had expected
that everything would be soaked through,
but she was unprepared for the thick layer
of smelly mud that covered everything.

'This is dreadful!' her mum said sadly.

'Everything's ruined. We're going to have to strip the entire kitchen and sitting room and start afresh.'

'It could have been worse. At least we're all safe,' Tyra's dad said soothingly, putting his arm round his wife.

They began discussing things like insurance and something called a 'dehumidifier', which would help to dry out the wet walls. Tyra decided to leave them to it. 'Let's try and find Jemima,' she whispered to Storm.

Storm nodded. He was invisibly sitting up with his front paws hooked over the edge of her bag.

Mud sloshed round Tyra's wellies as she went into the sitting room. She picked her way around soggy books, cushions and other stuff on the floor. There was

a musty smell of wet furniture.

Storm peered around curiously as if he couldn't imagine what the house looked like before the floods.

Tyra had a sudden thought. 'Could you use your magic to make our house as good as new?' she asked eagerly.

Storm blinked at her with serious midnight-blue eyes. 'Yes, I can do that

if you ask me to. But that would mean
giving myself away and then I would have
to leave.'

'Oh no. Don't do that! I never want
you to leave!' Tyra said hastily, wishing she
hadn't said anything. She couldn't bear
the idea of losing her friend. 'Mum and
Dad seem to be getting it all organized
anyway. I'm sorry I even asked. Let's just
try and find Jemima.'

Storm nodded.

Tyra kept looking, but there was no
sign of Shelly's doll. She was looking
behind the wet chairs and sofa, when she
spotted a scrap of pale blue material in the
mud. She pounced on it and picked it up.

'It's Jemima's hair ribbon! She must be
here somewhere,' she told Storm.

The tiny puppy leaned forward and

his little black nose twitched as he sniffed Jemima's scent. 'I will find her!' he woofed.

'No! Don't jump down! It's too wet and muddy in here,' Tyra said.

Storm grinned. 'My magic will protect me.' He leapt out of her bag, trailing a fountain of golden sparks behind him.

Squish! Tyra saw that there was something like a faint gold bubble starting to form around Storm's body, legs and paws. Splot! It hardened into something stretchy that changed shape with his movements as he began sniffing around. Blosh! Blosh! Storm scampered through the mud, but his fluffy fur stayed clean and dry inside the magical bubble.

'That's so amazing!' Tyra said, laughing. Storm looked cute and weird at the same time!

'What's amazing, love?' asked her mum
from the doorway.

'Um . . . the way the water's all
disappeared. Where's it . . . er, gone. You'd
never know it was like a swimming pool
in here a couple of days ago,' she babbled.

'I know,' her mum agreed. 'And, luckily
for us, in a few weeks' time it'll seem as
if the floods never happened. Any luck
finding Jemima?'

'Not yet,' Tyra said.

Out of the corner of her eye, she could see Storm ferreting around invisibly inside his glowing puppy-shaped bubble. She hid a smile, imagining the look on her mum's face if she could have seen him!

Tyra saw Storm making for the open front door. 'I'm going to look in the front garden. She might have got swept out there,' she said, following him.

'OK. But be careful where you're stepping,' her mum instructed. 'I'm just popping upstairs to get a few more things to take back to Pam and Mark's.'

Outside, Tyra picked her way round soggy plant pots and flattened flowers. She heard a muffled woof and looked over to see Storm scrabbling in a pile of

mud. He gave a triumphant yap as he
turned and bounded towards her. There
was something in his mouth.

'Have you found –' Tyra began, but she
broke off as she spotted the bedraggled
light-blue dress, the matted golden hair
and the doll's arm that was dangling at an
odd angle.

Chapter
SIX

The following afternoon, Tyra was curled
up on the sofa with Jemima on her lap
and Storm snoozing beside her. It was a
dismal grey day outside. Pam and Mark
were at work and Tyra's mum and dad
were in town, shopping for new furniture
and kitchen equipment.

'Poor old Jemima. I thought you were
lost forever,' Tyra said. She turned to

Storm. 'I'm so glad you found her. Thanks
again.'

'You are welcome.' Storm opened one
sleepy eye and yawned. Lifting his head,
he watched curiously as Tyra picked up a
brush and tried to untangle the doll's hair.

Tyra wasn't making much headway
with the brush. Jemima's once-bright
gold curls were dull and matted, and her
light-blue eyes were wonky and didn't
blink properly any more. Luckily, her dad
had managed to re-attach the loose arm.

Storm was just settling down again
with his fluffy paws tucked beneath him,
when Tyra heard the front door open
and close. There was a thud as Rachel
dumped her school bag in the hall.
Rachel's school hadn't been affected by
the floods as Tyra's had.

Storm jumped up, instantly alert. He stared across the room and wagged his tail as Rachel came in and walked towards him.

Rachel grinned at the cute puppy and stroked his soft little head. 'Hello, Storm! Nice to see you too.' She looked sideways at Tyra. 'Why are you sitting there cuddling that old doll? It's in a right mess,' she commented.

'As if I didn't know that!' Tyra said more sharply than she'd intended. 'I don't want to think about what Shelly's going to say when she sees her.'

Rachel rolled her eyes. 'According to you, Shelly's practically perfect. So she'll be fine about it, won't she?' she said. She flicked her dark hair over a shoulder and went out. Tyra heard her running up the stairs.

Tyra stared after her. 'Did you hear that?' she said to Storm, folding her arms across her chest. 'What's Rachel in a stress about now?'

'I think that Rachel seems like a kind person,' Storm woofed thoughtfully. 'She gave up her bedroom for you. I wonder whether she would really like to be friends, but is not sure how to tell you.'

'But I don't need another friend,' Tyra exclaimed. 'I've got Shelly and now you. In fact, you're all I need!'

A serious expression crossed Storm's little round face. 'I will not always be here. One day I must return to my home world and lead the Moon-claw pack. Do you understand that, Tyra?'

Tyra felt herself go cold. She couldn't bear to think of losing her magical little friend. 'Yes . . . but that won't be for ages, will it?' she asked, her voice catching.

'I will stay here as long as I can,' Storm woofed.

'That's all right then,' Tyra said, brightening. She gave him a cuddle.

But she couldn't help remembering how lonely she had felt before Storm arrived. *It might be nice to have another friend my own age, especially since Shelly will be living so far away*, she thought wistfully.

On Saturday morning, Tyra woke to find lemon-coloured sunlight pushing through the curtains. Storm was lying on his side, with all four legs stretched out. As Tyra reached over and began gently stroking his soft fawn-and-cream fur, his tail thumped against the duvet.

Tyra beamed at her tiny friend. 'How about a walk before breakfast?' she suggested, throwing back the duvet. Storm jumped down eagerly as she dressed quickly in jeans and a jumper. Tyra was going downstairs with Storm at her heels, when she heard voices from the kitchen.

'Have you made any plans for the

weekend?' Pam was asking Rachel. 'Why don't you and Tyra go for a bike ride or have a game of tennis on the Rec.'

'I don't think she's that bothered about doing stuff with me,' Rachel said quietly.

'Still not getting on too well? I thought that you two would make friends straight away,' Pam said. Her voice gentled. 'Give Tyra time. She's probably still upset about the flooded house and she's recently lost her best friend. She's bound to come round in time.'

Rachel sighed heavily. 'Oh well, I'll just have to think of something to do on my own, won't I?' Her voice grew louder as she came into the hall.

Tyra whipped round and shot back upstairs before Rachel spotted her. She felt slightly guilty for eavesdropping and

didn't want to get caught.

Storm followed her and then stood beside her on the landing. 'Is something wrong, Tyra?'

Tyra nodded as she realized that she been too busy moping about to notice that Rachel was feeling left out. 'I haven't been very nice to Rachel, have I? I feel bad about it. But I didn't mean to be horrible. I'm not usually like that.'

'I know that, Tyra,' Storm woofed, his bright eyes crinkling in a smile. 'If you were, I would not be your friend.'

Tyra smiled fondly at him. 'Thanks, Storm. I'm glad you understand. Do you think Rachel will give me another chance?'

Storm nodded, his tail twirling happily.

'How can I make up for being such a muppet?' she wondered aloud, and then a sudden idea jumped into her head. 'I know. How about if I ask *her* to play tennis with *me*? Oh no, I've just remembered. I can't. My racquet and tennis stuff is at our house . . .'

Storm's fluffy little round face lit up. 'That is not a problem!'

Tyra felt a familiar tingling sensation down her spine as bright gold sparks

glowed in his thick fawn-and-cream fur.
There was a whoosh of glitter that trickled
down round Tyra in a sizzling cascade and
tickled against her arms and legs.

Tyra looked down at herself. Her jeans
were gone and she was wearing shorts, a
white T-shirt and tennis shoes. She closed
her fingers round the handle of her tennis
racquet.

'Wow! Thanks, Storm. You're brilliant!' she said, smiling.

The last spark had only just faded from Storm's pale fur, when Rachel appeared at the bottom of the stairs. Her jaw dropped when she saw Tyra standing there in her tennis kit. 'What are you wearing that for?' she asked.

Tyra thought quickly. 'I was just about to come and find you. I . . . um, heard your mum telling my mum that you liked tennis. I thought you might fancy a game. There are tennis courts on the Rec, aren't there?' She swung the racquet about in a pretend volley, so that it made swishing noises in the air.

A pleased grin spread across Rachel's face. 'You bet! I'll go and get changed!'

Chapter
SEVEN

Tyra, Rachel and Storm wandered back across the Rec later that afternoon. Tyra felt hot and sweaty after an exciting afternoon of play. Both girls were good tennis players and were well matched, but Rachel had finally won by two.

Storm was weaving about, sniffing at things in the grass. He found something smelly and interesting and threw himself on to his back for a good roll. Picking himself up, he shook himself hard before gambolling after Tyra and Rachel.

Up ahead, Tyra suddenly spotted a group of teenage boys playing football. She felt a stir of unease as she recognized two of them: a tall thin boy and a shorter stocky boy with brown hair.

Rachel saw where she was looking. 'Uh-oh! There's Dale and Ed again. What a pain. Just ignore them and walk straight past.'

'I was going to,' Tyra said. She didn't think that Ed would be stupid enough to pick on her again. Not after Storm had taught him a lesson by making his hands go purple and swell up.

But she remembered how she had hurt her knee when Ed had shoved her against the slide and couldn't help feeling a bit nervous of the rough boys. Dale and Ed were both much bigger than her.

'Hey, Rachel!' Dale called out. 'Do you and your soppy friend need a puppy-walker?'

'Yeah! We'll come round and take Storm out for a walk sometime! We don't charge much,' Ed joked.

The other boys with them laughed and made hooting noises.

'As if!' Rachel shouted, sticking her

nose in the air.

Tyra swallowed hard, worried that the
boys would carry out their threat. She
just hoped that they didn't know where
Rachel lived.

Growing bored, Dale and Ed turned
back to their game. Relief washed
through Tyra. She was glad when they
reached the road and the teenage boys
were just small shapes in the distance.

'Ready for our bike ride then?' Mr
Carson said the following morning.

'OK then,' Rachel said. She pulled a
face at Tyra, who was sitting with Storm
on her lap. 'Dad's trying to keep fit. I have
to keep him company or he cheats and
calls into the café for a cake.'

'Me?' her dad said innocently.

Tyra laughed.

'We won't be very long,' Rachel said. 'Will you be all right by yourself?'

I could never be bored with Storm around, Tyra thought. 'I'll find something to do. No worries. Maybe I'll have another go at trying to smarten up Jemima, although it's probably a waste of time,' she said.

Rachel nodded and Tyra didn't see the thoughtful look on her face.

After she and Storm waved to Rachel and her dad as they cycled away, Tyra wandered back through the empty house.

Tyra's mum and dad were down at their house. Tyra hadn't fancied going with them this time. It was too depressing to see the downstairs rooms, now stripped of all furniture and carpets and looking horribly bare.

Pam was in the back garden. She
looked up as Tyra and Storm came
outside. 'Why don't you keep me
company?' she suggested. 'I could do with
a hand.'

'I don't mind,' Tyra said, smiling.

She wasn't that keen on gardening, but
she thought Storm might enjoy pottering
about in the fresh air, and she could leave
sorting out Jemima until later.

'You could do a spot of weeding, if
you don't mind,' Pam suggested. She gave
Tyra an old pair of gardening gloves and
then showed her a small plot with rows of
cabbages and other vegetables. 'It's mainly
tufts of grass that you need to pull up,' she
explained.

'No problem. I can do that.' Tyra
kneeled down and started work. The

your

spring sunshine was warm on her back.
Birds flitted about busily gathering
nesting material and two lime-green
brimstone butterflies fluttered overhead
in a spiral dance.

Storm snuffled about, exploring the
long grass, and then came to sit beside
Tyra. He watched her working for a
while, before bouncing down on to his
front paws. 'Grrr-ruff! He invited her to
play with him.

When Tyra didn't respond, Storm darted forward, scattering the pile of weeds on the path beside her. Grasping the cuff of her gardening glove in his sharp puppy teeth, he laid back his ears and tugged. 'Grr-rufff!' he insisted.

'Hey! Stop it, you pest!' Tyra scolded, laughing.

Pam laughed too. 'Storm's one determined little chap, isn't he?' she said, reaching out to pat the mischievous pup. 'You know, it's really lovely having him round the house.'

'I thought you didn't like dogs that much,' Tyra said.

Pam looked surprised. 'What makes you say that?'

'Well, Rachel's not allowed to have a dog, is she?'

'Oh, I see what you mean. I love dogs, but with all of us out of the house all day, it wouldn't be fair to have one,' Pam explained.

Tyra nodded agreement. 'No, it wouldn't. But Rachel's dead keen on Storm. If she had a puppy of her own, we could take them out for walks together.'

'I'm glad that you and Rachel seem to be getting on better now,' Pam said, smiling.

Tyra felt herself going red. She nodded. 'We didn't at first, but I think that was probably my fault,' she said honestly.

Pam patted her arm. 'Maybe – but it takes two to argue. Rachel can be moody too, even though she's got a heart of gold.'

Tyra nodded slowly. 'That's what Storm said . . . I mean, I could tell that Storm liked Rachel as soon as he met her,' she corrected hastily.

Luckily, Pam didn't seem to have noticed Tyra's slip-up. 'You know, I've been thinking about going part-time at the office for a while now. I think you've just helped me make up my mind.'

'Cool! So Rachel *could* have a puppy, couldn't she?' Tyra said eagerly.

Pam nodded. 'But don't say anything about this to her. All right?'

'OK!' Tyra agreed. She felt a tug on her jeans and glanced down to see that Storm was nibbling the hem. A giggle bubbled up from inside her. 'Is it OK if I finish off now? I think Storm really needs a walk.'

'Course it is.' Pam smiled. 'Thanks for your help. Leave those weeds there to dry out. I'll dump them on the compost heap later.'

Tyra stripped off her gardening gloves on her way towards the back door. Storm trotted along beside her. Tyra passed two bikes, which were leaning against the house wall. She went upstairs, intending to go to the bathroom to wash her hands.

As they reached her bedroom, Storm pricked up his ears. 'There is someone inside,' he woofed softly.

Tyra frowned, puzzled. She'd thought the house was empty, and then she remembered the bikes. Rachel and her dad must be back.

'I wonder why Rachel didn't come to find us,' she whispered.

As she went into the room, she saw that Rachel was bending over Jemima. She held the doll's silk dress in one hand and there was a pair of scissors in the other.

Tyra stared at her in shock. Her mind went into fast forward. It all suddenly made sense. Rachel was still jealous of Tyra's friendship with Shelly and she was about to take her anger out on Jemima!

Chapter EIGHT

'No – don't! Give her to me!' Tyra cried. She snatched Jemima away before Rachel could attack the doll with her scissors.

Rachel frowned in puzzlement. 'What's wrong?' she asked, and then her expression gradually changed as she realized what was happening. 'You thought I was going to cut up Jemima's dress, didn't you? As if I'd ever be that mean. Thanks a lot!'

'What were you doing then?' Tyra demanded.

'It doesn't matter now,' Rachel said bitterly. Her eyes glinted with tears. She got up and pushed past Tyra as she went out.

While Tyra stood there uncertainly, Storm jumped up on to the bed. He began nosing about on the duvet and then gave a triumphant woof as he made a grab for some things that were hidden in the folds.

'I can't believe Rachel. I really thought we were starting to be friends,' Tyra fumed, and then she frowned as Storm padded across the bed towards her with his mouth full of silky material and long trailing ribbons. 'What have you got there?' she asked him.

Storm dropped the objects in front of her. Tyra saw that the 'ribbon' was divided up into centimetres on one side and old-fashioned inches on the other.

'It's a tape measure. What would Rachel be doing with . . .? Oh no.' Tyra groaned as an awful thought occurred to her. She'd just made a huge mistake.

'I mentioned to Rachel that I was going to try and smarten Jemima up. I think she might have been going to make something for Jemima to wear! Now I've really done it. Rachel will never spoke to me again,' she said miserably.

The next few days were very busy. Tyra didn't see much of Rachel during the day as Rachel was at school. And most evenings, she and Storm went to the house with her parents. The dehumidifiers had worked really well and Tyra was happier being there as it was starting to look more normal.

On Friday evening, Tyra and Storm were returning to Pam and Mark's house after a visit to the pet shop. Tyra stopped to shift her bag on to her other shoulder.

It was full of tins of dog food and packets of treats and was heavy.

'I reckon we'll be moving home soon. Rachel will probably be pleased to have her bedroom back,' she sighed, feeling sad about how things had turned out between them. 'Anyway, Storm. You're going to love living there with me,' she said, cheering up a bit.

'Storm? Did you hear what I said?' she asked, looking down at him when he didn't answer her.

But Storm had stopped dead. Suddenly he gave a whimper of terror and shot through the nearest front garden gate.

Tyra frowned, puzzled. What was going on?

She dashed into the garden after Storm and was just in time to see him squirming under a hedge. Tyra bent down and peered in to where he was hiding behind a leafy branch. He had his tail tucked between his legs and was trembling all over.

'Storm? What's wrong?' she asked worriedly.

'It's Shadow. He has found me,' Storm whimpered. 'He has used his magic to send some fierce dogs to find me. Here they come now!'

Tyra heard a snapping and growling

noise from the street. She crept back
to peep round the gatepost and saw a
man approaching with two dogs. As she
noticed the dogs' fierce pale eyes and
extra long teeth, she caught her breath.

Quickly ducking back inside the
garden, Tyra crouched out of sight as the
dogs drew closer. The man struggled to
get them under control and finally led
them away. The growling noises faded as
he and the dogs turned a corner.

'It's OK. You can come out now,' Tyra
told Storm with relief.

Storm crawled out slowly, his fluffy
little belly brushing the ground. But his
eyes were still troubled and Tyra saw that
he was shaking.

She swept him into her arms and
stroked him gently as they went back out

to the street. She could feel his tiny puppy
heart beating fast. 'Those horrible dogs
have gone. You're safe now,' she crooned.

Storm shook his head. 'I will never be
safe now that Shadow knows where I am.
He will send other dogs after me. If they
find me, I may have to leave suddenly
– without saying goodbye.'

Tyra felt a sharp pang as she knew that
she would never be ready to lose him. 'If
that horrible Shadow gives up looking for

you, you could live with me for always!'
she burst out.

'That is not possible,' Storm yapped,
his little face serious. 'One day I must
go back to my home world and lead the
Moon-claw pack. Do you understand
that, Tyra?'

Tyra nodded reluctantly, but she refused
to think about that now. She just wanted
to enjoy every single moment spent with
Storm.

Chapter
NINE

The weekend dawned bright and clear.
Tyra was feeling in a pretty good mood,
considering that Rachel still wasn't
speaking to her. At least, there had been
no other signs of any fierce dogs and
Storm was back to his usual lively self.

Tyra, Storm and her mum were
wandering around the busy Saturday
market, while Rachel and her parents

were all in the indoor shopping centre.
Tyra had brought Jemima with her in her
shoulder bag.

'I might find a stall selling dolls' clothes
and I can buy Jemima a dress with my
pocket money. Maybe then Shelly won't
be so mad with me for getting her doll all
wet,' she whispered to Storm.

Storm nodded.

Tyra's mum paused at a stall to buy some flowers for Pam. Tyra wandered past her. She really wished that things were better between her and Rachel, especially as it was her own fault that they'd fallen out again.

'Hey! Look at that cute toy puppy, Storm. It looks just like you!' Tyra said, as she spotted a nearby toy stall. It gave her an idea. She took her pocket money from her jeans and quickly added it all up. 'I might buy that for Rachel,' she said on impulse.

'I think that Rachel would like that very much,' Storm yapped. 'But will you still be able to buy a new dress for Jemima?'

Tyra shook her head. 'No. I haven't

enough money for both. What shall I do? Could your magic help me?' she asked hopefully.

Storm put his head on one side. 'Magic cannot solve everything. I think that you must decide what to do yourself this time,' he woofed.

Tyra made a decision. 'You're right. Sorry, Shelly. Jemima will have to keep her old dress for now,' she said as she reached for the cute toy puppy.

Storm wagged his tail approvingly.

As Tyra was paying, she noticed a teenage boy in a red baseball cap looking at mobile-phone accessories on the next stall. He seemed to turn away quickly so that he had his back to her.

'That boy looks familiar. But I can't remember where I've seen him before,' she commented.

Storm glanced at the boy in the red cap. 'I do not recognize him either,' he yapped, with a doggy shrug.

Tyra lost interest in the boy as she walked away holding the toy.

The smell of frying onions and hot dogs filled the air. The market was getting busier. People of all ages, some with babies and others with dogs, filled the aisles between the stalls. Tyra started to worry that Storm would be stepped on. She bent down to pick him up. 'You'll be safer if I carry you.'

'Thank you, Tyra.' Storm sniffed the toy puppy and leaned forward to lick its fake-fur ears.

Tyra giggled and playfully took hold of his little muzzle. 'I don't think it needs a wash!'

As she turned round, she saw the lad in the red baseball cap again. He was facing her and Tyra felt a jolt as she recognized his thin face.

It was Ed, without his friend Dale this time, and he was staring hard at Storm. A chill ran through Tyra as the teenage boy came towards her.

'Aren't you a bit old for dolls and fluffy toys?' Ed scoffed, glancing at Jemima, who was poking out of Tyra's shoulder bag.

'What's it to you?' Tyra gulped in a wobbly voice.

She thought at first that Ed was going to grab Storm, but he hesitated, and seemed to think better of it, obviously remembering his supposed allergic reaction to the puppy. Suddenly, Ed swooped down and yanked Jemima out of her bag.

'Hey! Give her back!' Tyra ordered.

'What's it worth?' Ed crowed, raising Jemima in the air and about to throw her down on to the hard cobbles.

'No! She's made of china!' Tyra yelled, reaching up for the doll that the tall boy was holding out of her reach. But someone rushed up from behind and snatched Jemima out of his hands.

It was Rachel. 'Leg it!' she shouted to Tyra, already weaving away through the stalls towards a car park.

Tyra didn't need telling twice. She pounded after Rachel as if her feet had wings, and the two of them burst into peals of laughter at the sight of Ed scratching his head and staring after them.

She lost sight of Rachel for a moment

and paused next to some big delivery
vans. Suddenly Storm yelped with terror.
Wriggling out of her arms, he jumped to
the ground and sped between the vans.
At the same time, Tyra saw dark shapes
prowling towards her. They raised their
heads and she saw their abnormally long
teeth and fierce pale eyes.

Her heart missed a beat. They were here for Storm!

Tyra slid between the parked vans after Storm. Suddenly, there was a bright golden flash. Tyra blinked hard as her sight cleared. Storm stood there as his magnificent real self. The majestic young wolf's silver-grey fur gleamed and his midnight-blue eyes glowed like sapphires. A she-wolf with a gentle, tired face stood next to Storm.

And then Tyra knew that Storm was leaving her forever. She forced herself to be brave. 'Go, Storm! Save yourself!' she cried, her voice breaking.

Storm raised a large silver paw in farewell. 'You have been a good friend. Be of good heart,' he said in a deep velvety growl.

Tyra's eyes pricked with tears and there was a deep ache in her chest. She was going to miss Storm terribly. 'Goodbye, Storm. Take care. I'll never forget you,' she whispered hoarsely.

There was a final dazzling flash and a large silent explosion of sparks that crackled harmlessly down around her like warm rain. Storm and his mother faded and were gone. Tyra heard a frustrated growl and the fierce dogs instantly became normal and slunk away.

Tyra blinked back tears as she stood clutching the soft-toy puppy. At least she'd had a chance to say goodbye to Storm. She knew that she'd always remember her wonderful magical friend and the exciting adventure they'd shared.

Rachel appeared round one of the vans, still clutching Jemima. 'There you are!' she panted. 'Jemima's fine – no thanks to Ed!'

'Thanks.' Tyra took the doll and then held out the toy puppy. 'I thought you might like this until you get a real one.' *Which won't be too long now*, she thought happily, remembering her conversation in the garden with Pam.

'For me? Aw, thanks. It's gorgeous.' Rachel's eyes softened as she cuddled the toy.

'I'm sorry I've been such an idiot. Can we be friends?' Tyra asked.

Rachel nodded delightedly. 'Yeah! For keeps this time?'

'You bet!' Tyra said. Although she'd just lost one special friend, she now had a brand-new one. And her heart lifted because she knew that Storm would be really pleased about it.

Out Now

A little puppy, a sprinkling of magic, a fo ever friend . . .

Magic Puppy

Classroom
Princess

SUE BENTLEY

Coming Soon

Sparkling Skates   Sunshine Shimmers

APRIL 2008

puffin.co.uk

Magic Puppy

A New Beginning
9780141323503

Muddy Paws
9780141323510

Cloud Capers
9780141323527

Star of the Show
9780141323534

Party Dreams
9780141323794

A Forest Charm
9780141323800

Twirling Tails
9780141323817

School of Mischief
9780141323824

Snowy Wishes
9780141323831

Classroom Princess
9780141324791

Friendship Forever
9780141324784

Sparkling Skates
9780141324777

Sunshine Shimmers
9780141324760

A little puppy
a sprinkling of magic,
a forever friend

puffin.co.uk

A Summer Spell
9780141320144

Classroom Chaos
9780141320151

Star Dreams
9780141320168

Double Trouble
9780141320175

Moonlight Mischief
9780141321530

A Circus Wish
9780141321547

Sparkling Steps
9780141321554

A Glittering Gallop
9780141321561

Seaside Mystery
9780141321981

Firelight Friends
9780141321998

A Shimmering Splash
9780141322001

A Puzzle of Paws
9780141322018

A Christmas Surprise
9780141323237

Picture Perfect
9780141323480

A Splash of Forever
9780141323497

Win a Magic Puppy goody bag!

The evil wolf Shadow has ripped out part of Storm's
letter from his mother and hidden the words so that magic puppy
Storm can't find them.

Storm needs your help!

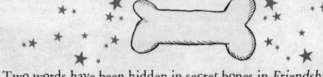

Two words have been hidden in secret bones in *Friendship Forever*.
Find the hidden words and put them
together to complete the message from Storm's mother.
Send it in to us and each month we will put every correct message
in a draw and pick out one lucky winner, who will receive
a Magic Puppy gift – definitely worth barking about!

Send the hidden message, your name and address on a postcard to:
Magic Puppy Competition
Puffin Books
80 Strand
London WC2R 0RL
Good luck!

puffin.co.uk